*For Anne and Vincent, Isis and Mandisa – M.H.*

*For Kenneth, Gwen, Nanette
and their families – C.V.W. and Y.H.*

First published in Great Britain in 1997 by
Frances Lincoln Children's Books, 4 Torriano Mews,
Torriano Avenue, London NW5 2RZ
www.franceslincoln.com

This paperback edition published in 2007

A catalogue record of this book is available from the Bristish Library.

ISBN 978-1-84507-874-4

Illustrated with watercolours

Set in Fairfield LH Medium

Printed in China

3 5 7 9 8 6 4 2

# An Angel
# Just Like Me

## MARY HOFFMAN

Illustrated by
CORNELIUS VAN WRIGHT & YING-HWA HU

**F**

FRANCES LINCOLN
CHILDREN'S BOOKS

It was nearly Christmas and everyone in the family was busy except for Tyler. Labelle and Marcy were putting up holly and ivy. Their mother and father had dragged in a big Christmas tree and T.J. was sorting through the old box of decorations. Even Simone was sticking paper chains together.

Tyler was the only one with nothing to do, so he teased Muffin.

"Oh no," said T.J. "Look at this angel!"

They looked.

"We'll have to get a new one," sighed Mum.

Tyler picked up the broken angel.

"Why do they all look like girls?" he asked. "Can't boys be angels?"

No one answered. Tyler just couldn't let it rest.

"Why are they always pink?" he asked. "Aren't there any black angels?"

"Good question," said his dad. "I never saw one, but then I never saw a real angel anyway."

"I'm going to find one," announced Tyler. "I'm going to get a new angel for our tree. One that looks just like me."

So every day, Tyler went into a different shop and looked at angels. Some were big and some were small, some were cheap and some were expensive. They all had wings.

But none of them looked a bit like Tyler.

None of the angels on the Christmas cards or wrapping paper looked like him either. Some played beautiful gold harps and trumpets. Some perched on rooftops or lolled on clouds. Lots of them were children and there were even some funny ones with skateboards or roller blades. But none of them looked like Tyler.

Tyler thought maybe Father Christmas could help.
All the big shops had one – but none of them looked
right to Tyler. Somehow, Tyler had always imagined
that Father Christmas would be a bit like his own dad.
    But all the Santas in the shops had curly white hair
and beards and red cheeks to match their clothes.

Except one. And he was at a shop where all the angels were as pink and gold as anywhere else. This Santa wore his beard like shaving cream on his brown face. He had a huge stomach. Tyler prodded it.

"Hi, Carl," he said. "Is that all yours?"

"Hi, Tyler," said the Santa. "No, it's a cushion. But you're not supposed to recognise me. This is my holiday job."

Carl was an art student friend of Tyler's parents and he sometimes looked after the children when Mum and Dad both had to work late.

Tyler told Carl his problem.

"I see," said Carl. "I never thought about that, but you're right. There should be angels like you."

"Oh well," said Tyler, "I suppose I'll just have to get a star instead. A star's the same for everyone."

On Christmas Eve, Tyler's family went to church. Inside, there was a crib with the baby Jesus and the animals in the stable. There were other figures too – a shepherd and some kings.

"Hey," said Tyler. "That king looks a bit like you, Dad."

But the angels were just like the ones in the shops, only bigger. And something else was beginning to bug Tyler too.

That night, before the children went to sleep, their mother read them the story of the first Christmas again.

"So Jesus was born in Bethlehem – and that's in Israel, right?" asked Tyler.

"Right," said Mum. "Nearly two thousand years ago."

"And Israel's a hot country, right?" said Tyler.

"Right again," said Mum.

"Then why doesn't the baby in the crib at church have dark skin?" asked Tyler. "It was as pale as all those angels I saw. Was that what the baby Jesus really looked like?"

"It's a good question," sighed Mum. "You're full of them this Christmas. But I don't know the answers. And if you don't go to sleep now, tomorrow's question is going to be, 'Where's our Christmas dinner?' Goodnight, Tyler."

On the other side of town, Father Christmas
was working late.

Christmas Day was always special at Tyler's house. There were two grandmas and one grandpa, an auntie and three cousins and even a visiting dog for Muffin to play with. It was as crowded as the crib in church.

Tyler looked up at the brand new gold star on the top of the tree and gave a little sigh.

"Stars are OK, aren't they?" said Dad. "Stars are the same for everyone."

"Yes," said Tyler, "But you can see stars in the sky most nights. You don't see angels. They're only for special occasions."

Just then, his Mum came in with a parcel.

"Late delivery from Santa," she told Tyler. "This just came through the letterbox for you."

It was the most beautifully carved wooden angel.
And – apart from the wings – it looked just like Tyler.

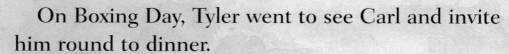

On Boxing Day, Tyler went to see Carl and invite him round to dinner.

"It was my best present," he told Carl. "Only now I want you to make something else."

"OK," said Carl. "What is it?"

"You see," said Tyler, "now my friends have seen my angel, they all want ...

... angels just like them!"

# MORE BOOKS ABOUT GRACE FROM FRANCES LINCOLN CHILDREN'S BOOKS

*Amazing Grace*
**Mary Hoffman**
**Illustrated by Caroline Binch**

Grace loves to act out stories. Sometimes she plays
the leading part, sometimes she is 'a cast of thousands'.
When her school puts on a performance of Peter Pan,
Grace longs to play Peter. Grace's Ma and Nana tell her
she can be anything she wants if she puts her mind to it.

*Grace & Family*
**Mary Hoffman**
**Illustrated by Caroline Binch**

To Grace, family has always meant her Ma, her Nana
and her cat, Paw-Paw, so when Papa invites her to visit him
in the Gambia, she dreams of finding a family straight out
of one of her story books. But, as Grace soon finds out,
families are what you make them.

*Princess Grace*
**Mary Hoffman**
**Illustrated by Cornelius van Wright and Ying-Hwa Hu**

Grace is back! The girl from *Amazing Grace* who proved
that you can be anything you want and that families are
what you make them, discovers that there's more than
one way to be a princess.

**Frances Lincoln titles are available from all good bookshops.**
**You can also buy books and find out more about your favourite titles,**
**authors and illustrators on our website: www.franceslincoln.com**